THE
TWISTED WITCH
and
Other Spooky Riddles

THE
TWISTED WITCH
and
Other Spooky Riddles

David A. Adler

illustrated by

Victoria Chess

Holiday House / New York

Happy birthday to Holiday House—
and to John
D.A.A.

Library of Congress Cataloging in Publication Data

Adler, David A.
  The twisted witch and other spooky riddles.

  SUMMARY: Dozens of riddles feature witches, vampires,
werewolves, ghosts, and other spooky creatures.
    1. Riddles, Juvenile. 2. Supernatural—Juvenile
humor. 3. Monsters—Juvenile humor. [1. Riddles.
2. Monsters—Wit and humor. 3. Halloween—Wit and humor]
I. Chess, Victoria, ill. II. Title.
PN6371.5.A327   1985   818'.5402   85-909
ISBN 0-8234-0571-0

When a witch lands, where does she park?

In a broom closet.

Do witches stay home on weekends?

No. They go away for a spell.

How does Dracula travel?

On blood vessels.

What are a vampire's favorite snacks?

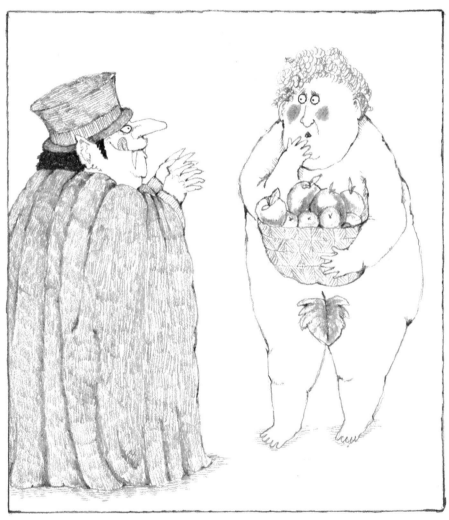

Adam's apples and nectarines.

What fur should you wear if you can't afford sable or mink?

Werewolf.

Why don't skeletons ski?

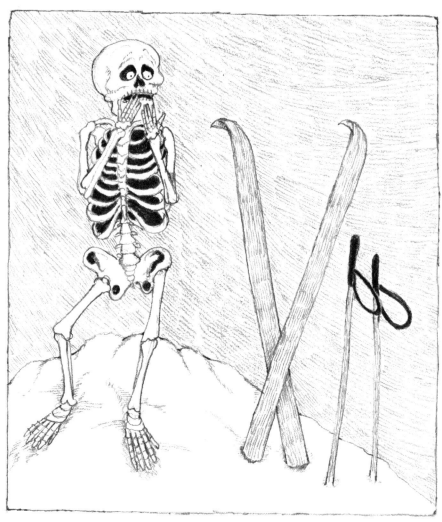

They don't have the guts.

What do you call a secondhand werewolf?

A wornwolf.

Why are so few ghosts arrested?

It's hard to pin anything on them.

What happened to the witch who hooked her broom to a space shuttle?

She got spaced out.

What happens to a fast witch on a slow broom?

She flies off the handle.

What would you get if you crossed a witch with an elephant?

I don't know, but she would need a pretty big broom.

What's worse than a witch without a broom?

A vampire with false teeth.

How are witches like an ugly bruise?

BOO

Witches are black and boo, too.

What do you get from a two-headed monster?

Double-talk.

How do you make a milkshake?

You sneak up behind a glass of milk and yell "Boo!"

What goes "Oob, oob?"

A witch in reverse.

What is covered with brown fur and flies?

A dead werewolf.

What if a vampire's teeth were twelve inches long?

They'd be fang footers.

What happens when a flying witch breaks the sound barrier?

You hear the broom boom.

When is it bad luck to see a black cat?

When you're a mouse.

What would you say if you saw Dracula's profile on a ten-cent coin?

Dimes have changed.

What should a taxi driver give a carsick witch?

Bus fare.

Where can you see a *real* ugly monster?

In the mirror.

What do demons do at night?

They go out with their ghoul friends.

What if you crossed a rabbit with a wolf?

You'd get a harewolf.

What did the bat say to the witch's hat?

You go on ahead. I'll hang around for a while.

How does a witch tell time?

She looks at her witch watch.

Where does Dracula keep his valuables?

In a blood bank.

Why don't skeletons like parties?

They have no body to dance with.

Can you tell me how long monsters should be fed?

Sure. The same as short monsters.

What time would it be if five demons were chasing you?

Five after one.

Why are mummies always late?

They get tied up.

Why do dragons sleep during the day?

So they can fight knights.

Which story do all little witches love to hear at bedtime?

"Ghoul Deluxe and the Three Scares."

In which forests do bats, demons and witches live?

Petrified forests.

Who has a broom and flies?

A jelly-covered janitor.

What's worse than being a 3000-pound witch?

Being her broom.

What would you find on a haunted beach?

A sand witch.

What's an overgrown vampire?

A big pain in the neck.

What did Dracula say when he saw a giraffe for the first time?

I'd like to get to gnaw you.

What would you call the ghost of a door-to-door salesman?

A dead ringer.

How do mummies hide?

They wear masking tape.

Why do witches think they're funny?

Every time they look in the mirror, it cracks up.

**What's the best way to stop the pain
of biting vampire bats?**

Don't bite any.

Why did the monster salute his vegetable soup?

He looked in his bowl and saw a kernel of corn.

How does a monster count to twenty-eight?

On his fingers.

What happened to the monster that took the five o'clock train home?

He had to give it back.

What's black and green, black and green, black and green?

A sick, twisted witch.

What do you call a ghost in a torn sheet?

A holy terror.

When do ghosts usually appear?

Just before someone screams.

What did the policeman say when a black widow spider ran down his back?

"You're under a vest!"

What's soft, moldy and flies?

A spoiled bat.

Why do cemeteries have fences around them?

Because people are dying to get in.

What do little ghosts drink?

Evaporated milk.

What should you say when you meet a ghost?

"How do you boo, sir. How do you boo."

What's a ghost's favorite breakfast?

Ghost toasties with booberries.